The Adventures of Finley Parker

The Race

Written by
Mallory Carruthers

Finley Parker's ready,

he's all geared up to go.

He has his **helmet on** and **shoes** to protect his toes.

Finn pushes the pedals
slowly,
the wheels begin to spin.

If he can pedal fast enough, there's a chance that **he could win!**

He pulls around the corner,

just past the willow tree.

The finish line is coming close,

the flag **he can almost see!**

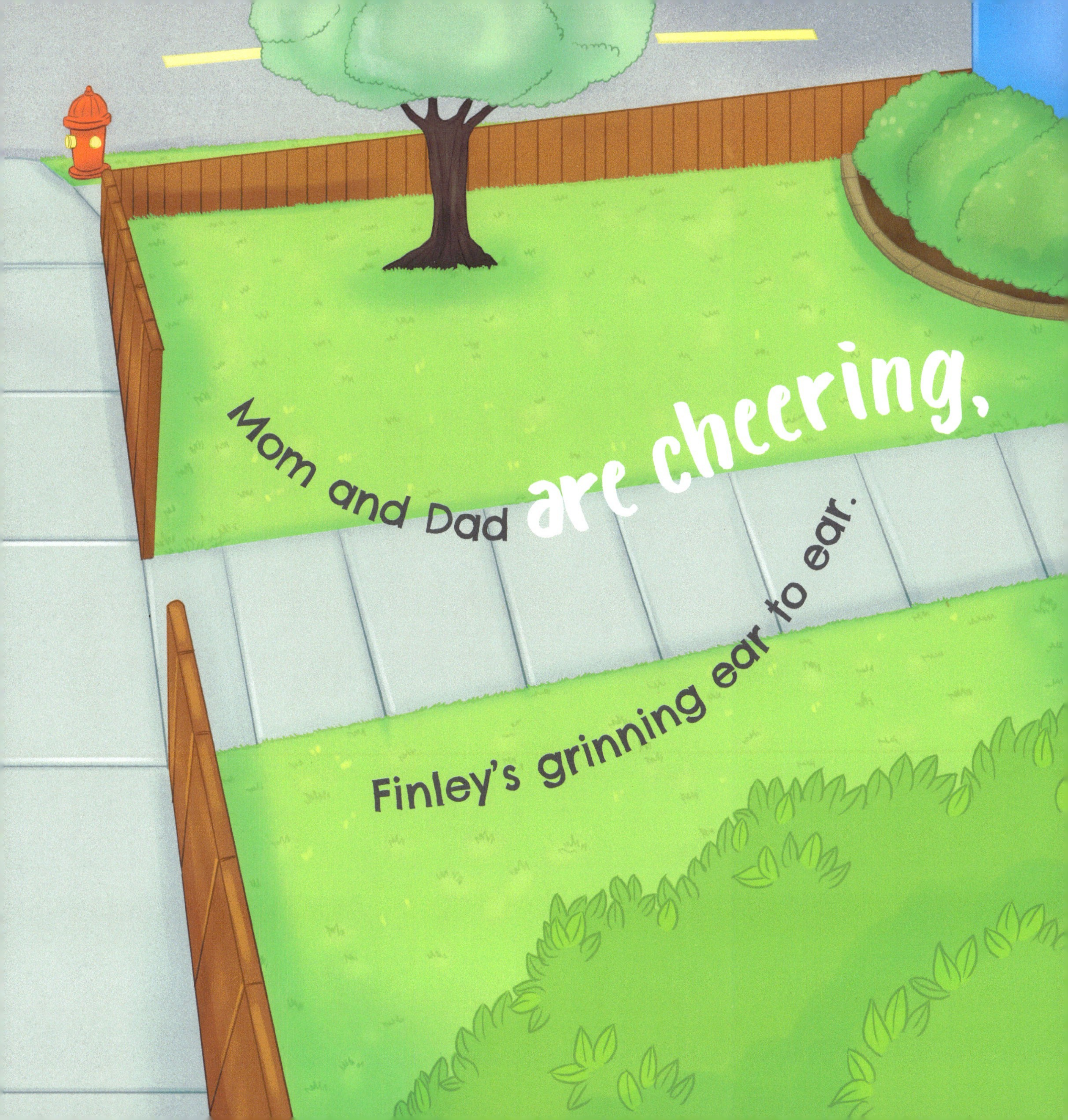
Mom and Dad are cheering,
Finley's grinning ear to ear.

He passes the line
and just in time...
The runner up is near!

Finn throws his hands up in the air.

Hooray for victory!

It was a great race...
Even though...

It was just
against a bee.

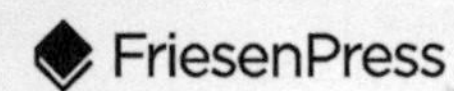

Suite 300 - 990 Fort St
Victoria, BC, V8V 3K2
Canada

www.friesenpress.com

First Edition — 2019

ISBN
978-1-5255-4874-1 (Hardcover)
978-1-5255-4875-8 (Paperback)
978-1-5255-4876-5 (eBook)

1. JUVENILE FICTION, FAMILY

Distributed to the trade by The Ingram Book Company

CPSIA information can be obtained
at www.ICGtesting.com
Printed in the USA
LVHW071555081119
636786LV00002B/18/P

* 9 7 8 1 5 2 5 5 4 8 7 5 8 *